This Welcome to School Book
is especially for

Wishing you many hours of
family reading fun and a
wonderful kindergarten year.

A gift from your school

 COMPLIMENTS OF
ECC PTA

Feathers
for
Lunch

Lois Ehlert

Voyager Books · Harcourt, Inc.
San Diego   New York   London

To Boots, Ibbi, Zuma Jay,
and the late Tom, Bucky, Cloudy, and The Chairman

My gratitude to Mark Catesby (1682–1749),
the Field Museum of Natural History, Chicago,
and the Milwaukee Public Museum

Requests for permission to make copies of any part of
the work should be mailed to the following address:
Permissions Department, Harcourt, Inc.,
6277 Sea Harbor Drive, Orlando, Florida 32887-6777.

First Voyager Books edition 1996
Voyager Books is a registered trademark of Harcourt, Inc.

The Library of Congress has cataloged the hardcover edition as follows:
Ehlert, Lois.
Feathers for lunch/Lois Ehlert.
p.   cm.
Summary: An escaped housecat encounters twelve birds
in the backyard but fails to catch any of them and has to
eat feathers for lunch.
[1. Cats—Fiction. 2. Birds—Fiction. 3. Stories in rhyme.]
I. Title.
PZ8.3.E29Fe   1990
[E]—dc20   89-29459
ISBN 0-15-230550-5
ISBN 0-15-200986-8 pb
ISBN 0-15-230551-3 oversize pb
ISBN 0-15-202662-2 pb NYSAEYC

Printed and bound by Tien Wah Press, Singapore

J I H G F E D C B

Printed in Singapore

Uh-oh.
Door's left open,
just a crack.

My cat is out and he won't come back!

geranium
plant

JINGLE
JINGLE

American Robin

TOMATO

He's looking for lunch,
something new,

JAY JAY
JAY

a spicy treat for today's menu.

JINGLE JINGLE

Blue Jay

pine tree

His food in a can
is tame and mild,

JINGLE
JINGLE

forsythia branch

Northern
Cardinal

WHAT
CHEER
CHEER
CHEER

bleeding heart
plant

so he's
gone out for
something wild.

House Wren

apple tree
branch

JINGLE JINGLE

He's snooping and sneaking — those birds sure look good.

Red-winged Blackbird

If he could catch one, he'd eat it, he would!

O-KA-LEE
O-KA-LEE

Rembrandt tulip

JINGLE
JINGLE

But when
his bell jingles,
birds call a
loud warning:

JINGLE
JINGLE

WHISTLE
WHISTLE
CHECK
CHECK
CHECK

Northern Oriole

lilac bush

WHO-O
WHO WHO
WHO

WHO-O
WHO WHO
WHO

Big cat got out early this morning!

Mourning Dove

JINGLE JINGLE

Northern Flicker

But cats
can't fly
and they
can't soar,

Ruby-throated
Hummingbird

JINGLE JINGLE
JINGLE JINGLE JINGLE

petunia plant

**and birds
know what
their wings are for.**

House Sparrow

CHIRP
CHEEP

forsythia
branches

So he keeps prowling, hoping to munch,

SU-WEE
SU-WEE

American Goldfinch

JINGLE JINGLE

but all
he catches
are
feathers
for lunch.

The lunch

SIZE: 7¼″–9″

FOOD: seeds, insects, small fruits, grains

HOME: woodland edges, thickets, gardens, parks

AREA: eastern United States, Arizona

Northern Cardinal

Northern Oriole

SIZE: 7″–8″

FOOD: insects, fruits, seeds

HOME: open woodlands, suburban shade trees, river groves, parks

AREA: throughout the United States and southern Canada

SIZE: 7½″–9½″

FOOD: insects, small fruits, seeds, grains, small aquatic life

HOME: marshes, hayfields, pastures, orchards, yards

AREA: throughout the United States and Canada

Red-winged Blackbird

that got away:

SIZE: 11"–12½"

FOOD: almost anything edible

HOME: suburban woodlands, gardens, towns, parks

AREA: eastern United States and central and eastern Canada

Blue Jay

American Robin

SIZE: 9"–11"

FOOD: insects, earthworms, snails, grubs, berries, seeds

HOME: cities, towns, farmlands, forests, gardens, backyards, lawns

AREA: throughout the United States and Canada

Mourning Dove

SIZE: 11"–13"

FOOD: seeds, grains, fruits

HOME: woodlands, gardens, parks, farms

AREA: throughout the United States and southern Canada

Ruby-throated Hummingbird

SIZE: 3¼″–3¾″

FOOD: flower nectar, tree sap, small insects, spiders

HOME: near flowers, gardens, woodland edges, orchards, parks

AREA: eastern United States and eastern Canada

American Goldfinch

SIZE: 4½″–5½″

FOOD: thistle seeds, insects, small fruits

HOME: near thistle patches, roadsides, open woods, orchards, gardens, parks

AREA: throughout the United States and southern Canada

House Sparrow

SIZE: 5½″–6¼″

FOOD: almost anything edible

HOME: farmlands, cities, towns, yards

AREA: throughout the United States and Canada

House Wren

SIZE: 4½″–5¼″

FOOD: insects, spiders

HOME: open woods, thickets, farmlands, towns, gardens, parks, orchards

AREA: most of the United States (except some southern areas) and southern Canada

Northern Flicker

SIZE: 11″–14″

FOOD: insects, berries

HOME: open woodlands, farms, towns, parks, lawns

AREA: throughout the United States and Canada

Red-headed Woodpecker

SIZE: 8¼″–9¾″

FOOD: insects, berries, sap, acorns

HOME: farmlands, orchards, wooded swamps, towns, gardens, parks

AREA: central and eastern United States and eastern Canada

All birds illustrated in this book, excluding those on the last four pages, are portrayed life size.